GHOSTS OF TEACHERS PAST

Also by Alexandria Blaelock

NOVELLAS
That Love Nonsense
Taipan vs Brown
The Ghost and Ms Cox
Friends Like That
Weaving the Wildwood
Wolf vs Orb

SHORT STORY COLLECTIONS
The Histories of Hayward Hall
Lovelorn, Lovestruck and Love at First Sight
Common or Garden Variety Heroes
Case Files of the Wilkinson Detective Agency
Unavoidable Fates
Christmas Travesties
Five Faces of Felicia Clarke
Little Place Called Home
Security Directorate Dossiers v. 1.
Security Directorate Dossiers v. 2.

MS BLAELOCK'S BOOKS
Stress Free Dinner Parties
Signature Wardrobe Planning
Holistic Personal Finance
Minimally Viable Housekeeping
Planning a Life Worth Living

PICTURE BOOKS
Australia Felix

SELECTED SHORT STORIES
Alan Ackerman is Still Missing
Alma's Grace
Blood and Bloody Profanity
Cancelled by the Cartel
Dingo Hunting
Honoris Virilis Respectu
Mince Pie Mystery

GHOSTS OF TEACHERS PAST

A SHORT STORY

ALEXANDRIA BLAELOCK

BlueMere Books

MELBOURNE, AUSTRALIA

For permission requests, please contact enquiries@bluemerebooks.com.

Ordering Information:
Discounts are available on quantity purchases. For details, contact orders@bluemerebooks.com.

Ghosts of Teachers Past/Alexandria Blaelock
paperback ISBN: 978-1-923083-34-9
digital ISBN: 978-1-923083-35-6

Book Layout © BookDesignTemplates.com
Cover Art © Liuzishan via depositphotos

GHOSTS OF TEACHERS PAST

Charity sat on the floor of the long, empty steel corridor, resting her back against the wall.

At least she thought it might be steel, because what else do you make space ships from?

Though for all she knew, it might be knitted from some kind of carbon fibre.

Or sculpted, hard-fired clay.

Or pixie dust.

She'd never been that good at the sciences.

Despite what other people said about their predictability, Charity found that numbers wriggle, and move, and change their meanings.

Just ask an accountant. What with the bank books, and shareholder books, and fundraising books, not to mention the tax books. The same sets of numbers prepared differently for different audiences.

No real wonder she never had any money in her books, which was why she was here on this stupid pixie dust boat headed home.

Words, on the other hand, were precise. If you need a word for some specific thing, there's bound to be one in some language or another from some time or another.

Like *ambage* (n) meaning equivocation, verbal trickery or deception.

From which we get *ambagitory* (adj), meaning indirect or circumlocutory language.

And *ambagical* (adj), meaning indirect or circumlocutory writing.

But if you can't find the right word, you can make up the exact combination of sounds to adequately express the concept. Like fantabulous, a combination of fantastic and *fabulous*. They both mean the same kind of thing, but this word adds a mythical dimension. Or maybe *fantastical* is a better word for that.

That's the thing about made-up words, you just keep going until you get the right one. And when you get the right one, you can covert it to a real one.

Charity's ship, AESV *Arcadia*, was built in the days when space ships were modeled on ocean ships, with definitive hull and upperdecks, bow and stern, port and starboard, forward and aft. First class at the top, third class at the bottom.

The walls of the corridor she sat in were once covered with a wood-panelling effect, though the thin laminate was chipped and peeling in places. The once red paisley-patterned carpet was now a kind of generic smudgy brown, threadbare in places.

No to mention that the air scrubbers didn't seem to work so well "down" here. The corridor smelled like curry and stale vomit left in a ground vehicle in the sun to dry.

It was pretty bad, but she was fairly sure there was a myriad of ways it could be worse.

Charity had booked her passage on the Seven Stars Space Line because of its old-fashioned glamour, and given the length of the trip, she thought she'd have lots of imaginary adventures.

It simply hadn't occurred to her that the cheap berths would be quite so ordinary.

Or that the ship would be quite so old.

Or that the glamour was pretty much limited to the somewhat more expensive "upper decks."

She'd watched that old *Titanic* vid, and the cheap rooms had been quaint and charming, but then again, the vid was made hundreds of years ago. And the original ship itself hundreds before that.

But just like then, she was sharing a room with a stranger. And that stranger was having loud sex in her room when she wanted a nap. They'd been at it for what seemed like hours.

If she ever caught another cruise liner, she'd spring for a private room.

Or perhaps she'd just go into cold sleep and post her capsule like a normal person.

Nothing so humiliating as failing and having to go back home. Years and years of humiliation at the family's hands to look forward to.

Her family wasn't exactly rich, though it wasn't exactly poor either. Charity didn't see why they couldn't have sent through a few thousand credits to be done with it.

It's not like any of them wanted her joining the family business. Wasn't it worth paying her to stay away?

Cheapskates all of them.

As the noise behind her rose to another crescendo, she started to wonder just how many people were in the cabin, and what the state of her bed was going to be when she finally got in there.

And couldn't they at least have made the gesture of inviting her?

Groaning, she forced herself upright and headed towards the Observation Lounge.

It was another classic steamship touch, a large transparent domed area on the "top" side of the mid-ship deck from which you could observe the stars.

Its dim lighting made it another popular place for amorous activities, but maybe this time of the rotation period she'd get lucky and find it quiet, if not empty.

The floor featured faded black and white checked tiles, with large potted fake plants placed at intervals. And a few rings where pots once stood.

The air conditioning simulated outdoor breezes, sometimes giving Charity the idea she could smell wide open spaces, not just air recycled so many times it was tainted by passenger halitosis.

On her way through the air-locked entrance, she stopped at a beverage dispenser and ordered water, which arrived lightly discoloured and cloudy in a slightly misshapen glass.

Perhaps next time, she'd choose a more modern ship as well.

Simulated cane chairs, *chaise longues* and occasional tables were arranged in small conversational groups, and she chose a chaise near the transparent external skin.

Some time later, she was startled awake by the sound of wings flapping.

Her cheap ticket included the bare minimum of entertainments; poker machines, a tired droid dance show and a vid theatre. The ship was human-habitat-only, and did not include an outdoor simulation let alone a living, breathing space, so wings, be they bug or bird-like creature were an anomaly.

Her first thought was she'd dreamed it, like some kind of omen or portent concerning her current situation.

And the second thought was *The Mayor of Casterbridge* by Thomas Hardy, specifically, the scene at the beginning where Henchard auctions his wife off, and a sparrow is trapped, fluttering around the tent trying to escape.

The wildly bangled, strawberry-blond haired, pre-Raphaelite styled Mrs Lawrence, Charity's English Literature, teacher had explained the trapped bird was a symbol of how poor Susan was feeling at the time.

An English Literature class had seemed like such a good idea at the time, and Charity had enjoyed it immensely. Diving deeply into stories and capturing all those hidden secrets had made her feel so very clever. But at the same time, not clever enough to write one herself.

The Mayor, as they called it, following Star Crossed Starships, *Sons and Lovers* (by Epping), and *Wuthering Heights* (Emily Brontë) as it did, was the last nail in the coffin of her belief that she *could* be a writer.

Book by book, the gloriously passionate literarian Mrs Lawrence had driven her authorial desires further and further, deeper and deeper down. So far, in fact, that after a time she ceased to remember a time when she thought she could be a writer.

But she still loved words, and reading, and talking about wonderful books. And for a while, thought she might even become a teacher like Mrs Lawrence, so she could share her love of books.

Mrs Lawrence was an inspiring teacher, who arrived at a crucial point in Charity's life. But as time passed, Mrs Lawrence felt like more and more of a nut-job, and eventually teaching was no longer an option. Let alone teaching passionate Mrs Lawrence style.

She'd settled for librarianship.

It's funny how a really great teacher never leaves you. Anytime you find yourself in some kind of dilemma, you can close your eyes, cast your mind back and ask them for advice.

Not a theoretical kind of thing like what would Jesus do, but a full-on conversation with the teacher of your choice.

What would Mr Fuller, your science teacher say? Or Art 2B's Mrs Green? Mr Goes from Higher Mathematics?

Just like the dead people you know, that handful of excellence stalks your waking life, stops you messing up and having too much fun.

At a crucial point, where a life-changing decision needs to be made, you'll see Mrs Green turn a corner right in front of you.

Or Mr Fuller shakes out and refolds his reproduction broadsheet newspaper from the seat diagonally opposite you on the bullet transit. An amazing feat of ingenuity, and as a tool for impressing the less dexterous it's the only reason why anyone prints broadsheets.

You don't even need a psychic to contact the teachers (assuming you could find one willing to try). No matter where you are in time and space, they're right there with you.

All you have to do is look for them.

Charity kept her eyes closed while she listened again, trying to decide whether the creature was there, or it was the remnant of a dream. Or perhaps whether some cut-throat or footpad had turned up to threaten her with menaces.

The Observation Lounge seemed still and quiet to her hyperactive ears, so she opened one eye and looked around. She was lying on her side, ostensibly observing the stars, and she didn't see anything untoward, so she opened the other.

Swivelling her head, still nothing, but that wasn't really helping with what was going on behind her.

Spine tingling, she pushed herself upright.

Something moved in the corner of her eye, but when she turned, there was nothing to see. She shivered a little, remembering the *Sparrow*.

The story of the abandoned ship, floating alone and empty through space for more than a century had intrigued her for years. What happened to the crew? Why had they left their dinner? Where did they go?

Growling, she shook herself to dispel her doubts and built up tension.

And after checking the time, walked to the Dining Room for some breakfast.

As she ate, she thought about her experience in the Lounge.

Was the noise an indication the air conditioning was malfunctioning? Or had there once been a holographic simulation that was worn out, but still active?

She decided to check the Ship's Library to see what she could find out.

After retrieving her tablet, she returned to "her" chaise in the Observation Lounge with a simulated coffee, which tasted weirdly better than the water.

Logging in, she spent happy hours trawling the net looking for information about the ship.

It was old.

Really old.

So old, in fact, it was one of the original Seven Stars Line spaceships. Way back from before the time when people were comfortable travelling and living in space.

Though it had been refurbished so many times, it was unlikely any of the original ship remained.

But each time it was made over, it was done in such a way it stayed almost exactly the same.

It remained a "classic," never modernised, and marketed to history buffs as a way to step back in time to the Golden Age of space travel.

Charity snorted. Golden Age her *derrière*.

But more interestingly, the Observation Lounge was originally a live habitat, with living plants, insects and birds. Interlinked ponds provided water for the creatures as well as a reservoir for the fountains and concealed misters for watering the plants.

The dome had regulated a ship-wide planetary cycle; opaque blue with a rotational sun during the diurnal phase, nocturnally transparent for stargazing, mediated by "sunrise" and "sunset."

Programmed air currents blew through the foliage, dispersing the scent and sound of live plants to make planet-bound passengers more comfortable during long trips.

And supplemented the air recycling with fresh oxygen and carbon.

Sadly, in those days, they hadn't known of or mapped the radiation fields, and the ship was caught in one. It killed everything on board and triggered the auto-recall before they'd realised the danger.

The ship had been thoroughly cleaned and fitted with stronger shields before recommissioning, and the live habitat restocked.

But something went wrong, and it weakened and died out.

As did the third and fourth live habitats, though no one could figure out why.

The Seven Stars Space Line installed a holographic simulation to replace it, and it had worked well for decades, but one by one the projectors failed, and as the ship's technology was incompatible with the technology of the day, the system was switched off.

Though according to some reports, the projectors still fired off randomly here and there.

Charity wondered if they'd intended to replace the holographic system during the next major refit, or whether they planned to scrap the vessel.

She saved her search results, then lay back, tablet resting on her belly, and stared through the transparent dome trying to imagine what the ship had been like when it was brand new and freshly commissioned.

Were the tickets very expensive as befitted a brand-new luxury ship?

Or cheap enough to entice intrepid young daredevil travellers?

She closed her eyes to better picture a planetscape she'd never experienced in person. Blue sky overhead, trees and gardens waving in a gentle, sunshine scented breeze. Brightly coloured birds swooping between the trees chirping, buzzing insects flitting here and there.

Now and again, the chink of ice-filled glasses being lifted, and cutlery scraping across plates. Polite conversations in archaic, but understandable Earth Standard *lingua franca*.

Her imagination was so vivid, when she opened her eyes, she could see a young couple in reproduction ship suits strolling the gardens. They nodded at her as they passed by.

She didn't remember seeing any mention of historical re-enactment in the ship's daily bulletin of activities, but if she had, she'd have signed up immediately.

Did they own their costumes, or was there a hire-shop on board?

She stood to go after them, but they had disappeared.

As had the historical simulation.

The Lounge was as distastefully old, fake and dingy as she'd first found it.

She sat down again, strangely disappointed to find it wasn't real.

Had she dreamt it? Was she dreaming now?

She pinched herself and yelped in pain and surprise.

Probably not dreaming then.

Could she be hallucinating?

She'd passed her last mental fitness check with flying colours, so that wasn't real likely. But it was possible the air or water recycling systems were inadequately cleaning the air or water, and that some kind of hallucinogenic substance was cycling through.

Though as far as she knew, it wasn't possible to control hallucinations, and they were rarely germane to the lived experience.

But if it wasn't real, what the hell was it?

According to her recent research, the holographic system had been inoperative for decades, so not a ship-generated experience.

If it's not science fact, she heard the ghost of Mr Fuller say, it must be science fiction.

Seeing no reason to doubt him, she scanned her memory of pulp fiction and came up with ghosts, time travel and some kind of direct attack on her person.

Unable to think of anyone who might want to harm her (aside from her family who were more likely to wait until she got home to launch a direct attack), let alone knew that she was on this particular ship, and in a position to attack, she was left with ghosts and time travelling back to the Golden Days.

Neither of which seemed like a situation she wanted to be a part of.

The technology for time travel did not, so far as she knew, exist.

Which left ghosts.

And ghosts, it was generally accepted, became ghosts due to the trauma of their deaths.

Or in an attempt to finish unfinished business.

You didn't often hear about haunted ships or space stations by comparison to planets. Did that mean that something about terrestrial surfaces was more compatible with ghosts? Or something to do with space stations and vehicles having a standardised "daylight" interior.

Mind you, these days dark vehicles were generally deemed hostile, contagious or derelict and shot up in a preventative strategy so there wouldn't be many ghost reports originating from those vessels.

Regardless, the sensible thing seemed to be to avoid the Observation Lounge and find some other place for napping.

Charity thought that was the end of the matter, but only a few days later, she started seeing and hearing the birds in other areas of the ship.

The Promenade deck, the Dining Room, the Games deck.

Areas that were not equipped with holographic projectors.

She started seeing the nodding couple reflected in the shopping mall windows, but when she turned to acknowledge them, they were gone.

And then she saw them in the corridors.

It was ridiculously exciting, like a grown up version of hide and seek.

When she started looking for them, she saw them more often. Following them, but as the corridors filled with people, the couple turned a corner and disappeared.

She wondered who they were, and she started looking through the ship's image collection. Judging by their ship-suits, they were within the first few decades of its travels, so she started there.

Eventually, she found them. Young Mr Caleb and Mrs Hope Cafos on the shuffleboard court, a few days before the ship found the radiation cloud.

She examined it closely. They looked happy in their vintage ship-suits, leaning on their cues in the midst of a field of discs, laughing at whoever was taking the picture.

Creepy.

So why was she seeing them now?

What were they trying to tell her?

She'd been idly flicking through the images, since she'd seen the Cafos', not really seeing them when something tweaked her brain, and she had to go back several images to see what it was.

It was her.

Miss Charity Vere, in a vintage ship-suit, playing mini-golf.

Not just someone who looked like her, but someone who had her name as well.

What the heck?

She looked through more pictures, more closely, examining the people in the fore and background, and saw the three of them in the Observation Deck, eating something that looked like cake with a pot of something that could be tea.

Freaky.

The three of them walking the Promenade deck.

The three posed with lifebuoys in the main lobby.

Was it possible the three of them had travelled together?

Why was "she" travelling with them?

She saved her searches and shut down her tablet.

It seemed like she had no choice but to find them and demand an explanation.

If that was even possible of ghosts.

She squared her shoulders and headed towards the Observation Lounge, though her steps slowed as she got closer until she paused outside the door.

You can do anything you set your mind to, Mr Goes whispered in her ear.

And yet she'd never quite got Higher Mathematics no matter how hard she tried.

Mrs Green pushed roughly passed her, and without hesitation, entered the Lounge.

Charity swallowed her doubts and opened the door.

Her tablet slipped unnoticed from her hands as she walked over the threshold.

As soon as she crossed over, the original live garden grew up around her.

"Charity, where on earth have you been?" Hope demanded.

"I... I... I was looking for you silly! Where's Caleb?"

"He went to find you, but I expect he'll be back in a minute."

"I'm sorry I'm late, I got lost. These endless ship corridors all look the same - they should add some kind of colour coding system."

"Maybe they'll do that for the next one. Oh, look, there's Caleb." Hope stood and waved at her husband.

He kissed them both on the cheek before sitting down, "Did you order? I'm starving."

"Of course darling, it's on the way," Hope replied.

Charity knew there was something important she needed to ask them, but she couldn't remember what.

"I'm so glad we're all here together," Caleb said, "we're about to enter some kind of energy field, and they say the view is going to be spectacular. I'd hate for any of us to miss it."

"That's so exciting," said Charity, "I wouldn't want to miss it for the world."

«« • »»

The Vere's were not happy when they discovered Charity had disappeared during the voyage.

For one thing, the Seven Stars Space Line could have notified them, so they didn't need to bother going to the port to collect her.

As Charity was known to spend a lot of time in the Observation Lounge, and her tablet was found just outside it, Seven Stars assumed she was in there when the Dome blew and was sucked out into space.

They were very apologetic, refunded her ticket price and made a compensatory payment for her death.

Her belongings were packed up, and the family took them with little ceremony and threw them into a storage locker without looking at them.

As the generations passed, she became a family myth.

Another ship wreck victim to add to those the family lost in the *Lusitania, Caronia, Proxima, Symphonia,* and *Xena.*

THE END

As a small token of my thanks for reading...

Please enjoy 10% off everything (excluding shipping)

at alexandriablaelock.com

with the code charityten.

Turn the page for some ideas where to use it,

If you enjoyed this story, why not try the collection?

Is the future something to look forward to?

Utopian or dystopian? A place where the greater good outweighs individual concerns, a place where life and death is a matter of the choices you make, or a place you have to walk away from?

Whether it's good or bad, the future is what you make it.

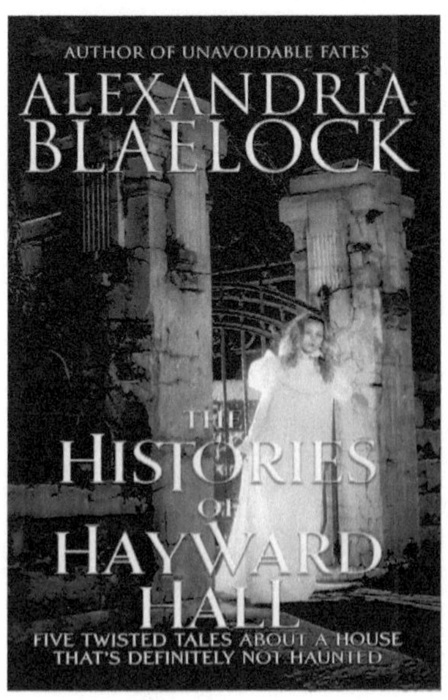

Meet Morag Clementine. The new housekeeper at historic Hayward Hall.

Her practical and capable attitude usually keeps her out of trouble.

bove all, her no-nonsense, get it done approach. And her get in the middle of the scrum outlook. Just as well, because Hayward Hall needs someone like her.

In this genre-spanning collection of original stories, Morag finds herself ensnared in the History of Hayward Hall...

No ordinary housekeeper, can Morag save the house, one century at a time?

Do you have what it takes to be a hero?

Whether that's running into a burning building, standing up for what you know is right, or saving the Princess it's going to take everything you've got and more besides.

In this genre-spanning collection of original stories, five women draw on resources they didn't know they had.

Join them, if you dare.

Bitter and Sweet. Dark, nutty or plain.

If Christmas under the hot Australian sun isn't twisted enough, these stories turn it up a notch or ten.

This collection is like a box of Christmas chocolates, there's something for everyone!

you go girl!
The opposite
of winning
isn't losing,
it's quitting.
· Martha Rosette Lutz ·
Time for
a nice cup
of tea and
a sit down
Time for
a nice cup
of tea and
a biscuit
there's a book
for that

Time for a nice cup of tea
and a sit down

BEWARE THE EMPTINESS GREMLINS

ABOUT THE AUTHOR

Australian author Alexandria Blaelock writes mostly fantasy and mystery.

She's appeared in the Stringybark Anthology *Crowd Surfing*, *Pulphouse Fiction Magazine*, and *Ellery Queen's Mystery Magazine*.

She's also written five self-help books applying business techniques to personal matters like getting dressed, tidying up, and feeding friends.

Discover more at alexandriablaelock.com.